Steam Room

Dre D'eshon

TABLE OF CONTENTS

1

"Stay Away From The Steam Room!"

"Are you sure about this, ma'am?"

The gangly-faced driver glanced at her through the rear-view mirror for the thousandth time, his forehead creased with worry lines. Sitting in the backseat of the Escalade, Ashley McBride let out another sigh and rolled her eyes.

"For the last time, Eddie, yes," she told him. "I am more than sure that this is the place I wanted you to bring me to."

Ashley raised her hand to her face, staring at the gleaming ring on her finger for a few seconds. She dropped it and gazed out the window at the tall building, trying to not to lose her calm as pedestrians walked by and momentarily blocked her view. The building wasn't much to look at. It was old, with bricks jutting precariously out of the walls and cracks in the large windows. She couldn't see much through though the glass panes, but she thought she spotted people moving around. Hanging right over the glass entrance door, dusty and chipped, was a large sign that read: *'DEZ*, FITNESS AND EXERCISE.

If it weren't for that sign, she might have assumed it was some sort of hideout for robbers or something.

"Yeah," she muttered, suddenly unsure of herself. "This is the right place."

Edward twisted in his seat and looked directly at her. "Ma'am, this place is a dump. I bet there are better gyms in Manhattan. Are you sure you don't want me to drive you over to one of them? It'd only take ten minutes. This...this is no place for a woman like you."

She fixed him with an amused look. "Why? Because of Matthew? Are you concerned about me or your boss's reputation?"

The driver gaped at her, unable to form words, and turned away slowly.

Ashley felt a smirk tug at her lips. Being the wife of a millionaire definitely had its perks. For one, she didn't have to drive herself around, which was a relief considering the fact that although she knew how, she didn't really like it. She still worked in sales, even though she didn't have to anymore. And she had enough money to spend on year-long vacations. It was, to put it quite simply, heaven.

But it wasn't perfect. Matthew was everything she'd always dreamed of marrying: rich, handsome, and generous. Sadly, that was all he was. In bed…well, Ashley didn't like to think about the time they spent together in the bedroom. It didn't matter as long as he loved her and showered her with gifts, right?

Right?

Wrong. As much as she'd thought she could handle the fact that he was a disaster in bed, she really couldn't. And so, just last week, while they were returning home from a function, she'd announced that she wanted a divorce.

Still, that hadn't been enough. Ashley needed something more in her life. She wanted fun, excitement…*passion*. And so she'd gone to the only person who could possibly help her.

Ciara had been thrilled to help her best friend, which was no surprise since she'd never really thought much about Matthew. No sooner had the words left Ashley's mouth than the other woman started mentioning places in Manhattan where she could find what she was looking for.

Not that many of these places had been helpful, anyway, Ashley thought, remembering the night she'd walked into a bar looking for a strapping man to fuck and had instead met old men with greying beards and raspy voices. She'd gone to all the places Ciara advised her to.

All except one.

She looked out at the building again, wondering what she might find when she walked inside. It was supposed to be filled with people pumping iron, right? Hopefully, this wouldn't be like the night at the bar. Ashley wanted young, sexy men; scraggly beards and Alzheimer's weren't much of a turn-on for her.

But if the sort of men she wanted were in there, she'd never find out unless she checked out the place. Ashley couldn't afford to hesitate any longer. She was twenty-nine, and she hadn't had a proper orgasm in years. She needed to *fuck*.

She tugged the ring off her finger and stuffed it into her bag. She wouldn't be needing that today.

"You don't need to wait around for me," she told Edward, pulling her blonde hair into a ponytail.

She saw his eyes widen in the rear-view mirror. "But, ma'am –"

"I'm perfectly capable of finding my way back home, Eddie," she snapped. She grabbed her bag and was reaching for the door handle when a sudden thought hit her. "Oh, and if my husband asks where

I went, tell him I went to hang out with Ciara for a bit, okay?"

The driver nodded slowly. Ashley could see the confusion in his eyes, but as much as she'd have loved to be honest with him, she couldn't. It wouldn't exactly help her already crumbling marriage if Edward let it slip to Matthew that his wife was searching about for random strangers to fuck her brains out.

"Thanks." She flashed him a brilliant smile and climbed out of the car, hoping she hadn't overdressed for this. She was wearing neon-green sports bra with pink sweatpants, a pair of rather flashy Nikes on her feet. Around her head and wrists were white bands. Oh, and there was the extra set of clothes in her bag.

As long as she didn't attract too many mocking stares, she was fine with that. Ashley waved at Edward, who nodded and rolled up the windows, driving out of the street in seconds. Heaving a sigh, she turned to face the building, staring up at the sign.

"Let's hope this goes well," she muttered, and pushed the door open.

The building was, surprisingly, a lot more presentable on the inside than it seemed from outside. She had to admit, it was pretty good. Neat, to begin with. And from the look of things, it had enough equipment. But her attention was focused on one thing and one thing only: the men.

They came in all shapes and sizes, moving from benches to dumbbell racks to treadmills. From what she could see, though, not all of them were as good-looking as she'd been hoping, and she doubted they'd be good in bed. Plus, a number of them were much older than she would have preferred. Several men looked up when she walked in, some pausing their exercise routines to get a good look at her. Ashley saw a couple of women working out in a corner, conversing softly. They locked eyes with her and scowled, giving her a cold once-over, then resumed chatting like nothing had happened.

Just then, Ashley's phone buzzed in her pocket and she fished it out, staring at the screen. It was a message from Ciara. She opened it and READ:

You there yet, girl? I bet you've found yourself a good guy to take you down town already. ☺

Ashley grinned. *I wish.* Sure, there were a couple of good-looking guys in here, but she just wasn't attracted to them in any way, starved as she was. She gave a start as another message came in:

One more thing: STAY AWAY FROM THE STEAM ROOM!

She gave a frown. That was new. Was there something about the steam room she was supposed to know about? Or was Ciara just worried she'd get stuck in there with a dozen guys with extremely hairy chests?

Right as she was about to send a reply, a hand touched her arm. She jumped in surprise and spun around. Standing before her, dressed in a striped blue tracksuit, was a man who looked like he might be in his early forties. He had slightly greying hair and a smile that seemed a bit too wide for his face.

"Hi," he said. "I'm Fernandez, but you can call me 'Dez. I run this place. Is there any way I can help you?"

Was it just her, or were his eyes drifting towards her breasts every couple of seconds?

"I believe there is," she responded. "I'm not sure where to start."

Fernandez grinned. "Ah. You'll be wanting to start with the treadmill. Get those beautiful legs of yours pumping, you know." He had a throaty voice and a light accent, which didn't match his looks at all. He pointed at the nearest vacant treadmill. "That one's free."

Okay, he was definitely ogling her.

"Thank you." She flashed him a sweet smile and made for the treadmill, setting her bag down. She could feel several eyes on her as she began exercising, starting with a walk and then breaking into a light run, her breasts jiggling like crazy, threatening to burst free from the sports bra.

In a flash, Fernandez was standing by the machine, grinning at her.

"You look real good, lady," he told her. "Where do you work?"

"Nowhere important," Ashley panted. She stopped the treadmill and faced Fernandez, setting both hands on the handle. "Look, I know you want to fuck me."

The man's eyebrows shot up like they were trying to hide from her. Clearly, he hadn't been expecting her to be so blunt. "Well, you *are* very attractive."

"I know. But here's the thing: I'm not attracted to you, so it's best you understand now that you and me, we're never going to fuck. Do you understand?"

Fernandez nodded slowly, surprise still on his face.

"Good." She gave him another smile and extended a hand. "I'm Ashley. Nice to meet you."

He shook it, still stunned. Then his lips slowly curved upwards. "Just let me know if you ever need anything."

"As a matter of fact, I do…where's the steam room?"

Ashley had just remembered Ciara's message about the room. For some reason, it made her more curious than wary. What could possibly happen if she *did* go to the steam room? She'd get pounded by hairy dudes? That didn't sound like such an awful thing.

Fernandez pointed. "Over there. Go through that door, first, get undressed, grab a towel from the rack on the wall to your right. You'll find the steam room three doors to your right."

"You're such a kind man," she told him, touching his arm lightly. With that, she left the machine and, following his directions, came to a stop just outside a door. She pushed it open and was hit in the face by a blast of steam. Clutching the towel tighter around her, she stepped into the steam room.

It was smaller than she'd expected, but big enough, anyway. It was hard to see through the steam, but Ashley took note of the tiled walls and mounted marble benches. The temperature was way higher than it was outside, but she didn't mind; it was just steam and a bit of wetness, after all. It wasn't like it could burn her. She looked around, peering through the steam for a sign of anyone else, but from what she could tell, she was very, very alone.

"Perfect," she muttered, taking a seat and leaning heavily against the marble tiles. She wasn't sure why she was so disappointed. It wasn't like seeing hairy guys in here would've been any better. She figured it was because the whole thing, dressing up and coming to the gym, had been pointless. So many guys, yet not one of them was what she was looking for.

"Damn you, Ciara," she groaned aloud.

The room seemed to grow hotter, and Ashley decided to take off her towel. What better way to enjoy the steam? Besides, she was the only one in the steam room. Without another thought, she pulled the towel off her, setting it down beside her on the bench, and parted her legs wide, her eyes closed, sighing as the steam hit her bare skin. On a sudden thought, she ran her hands between her legs and began caressing her core, feeling the sensations zing through her body. Oh, God, it felt so good…

"Now, there's something you don't see every day," said a voice.

Ashley nearly jumped out of her skin. Sitting across the room from her, watching her with a look of pure amusement on his handsome face, was a man.

2

"Want To Touch Me?"

He'd been there the whole time. Ashley couldn't believe she hadn't seen him through the steam when she entered the room. She kept her eyes on the man, her eyes widening to the size of saucers.

There's a man in the room.

It didn't help that he so damn gorgeous.

For a few seconds, all she could do was stare at his face. He was dark-skinned, with even darker eyes that seemed to see right into her. Bushy eyebrows rose slightly as he met her gaze. His face was chiselled, like he'd been specially sculpted or something. And his lips? Ashley wasn't sure she'd be able to maintain control of herself if he touched her with those pink lovelies. Staring at him, she could feel her nipples hardening, turning into swollen rosy buttons.

Her gaze slid down, past his thick, muscular neck, and settled on his chest, which was sprinkled with just the right amount of hair. His pectorals…well, it didn't quite ease Ashley's sudden palpitations to see how bulging they were. She shifted her gaze to his arms, which were thick, somewhat veiny, and his large, powerful-looking hands. Ashley figured he must lift a lot of things, even outside of the gym. No one else at *Dez* was this sexy.

When she finally settled on his abs, she thought she might have a sensory overload. This was no man. This was a god.

Ashley could only imagine what this god was packing in the sack.

She made a strangled sound in her throat, suddenly finding it hard to breathe. Finally, she found her voice. "It's rude to stare, you know."

The man grinned again, crinkles forming around his eyes, and Ashley figured he must be in his late thirties. Then, all of a sudden, he looked away, amusement still etched on his face.

"Sorry," he said. His voice was thick and effortlessly sexy. "It's not every day one sees such a sexy woman get nude in the steam room."

His words sent a shiver racing down her spine. *He* thought she was sexy? She'd only been slightly flattered when the other men and Fernandez ogled her, but a compliment from a hunk like this was enough to turn her bones to mush. She felt a tingle between her legs, and her breathing quickened a little.

She bit her lip, wondering if she should put the towel back on, but decided it didn't matter. After all, he'd already seen her naked body. Besides, he found her attractive. Ashley couldn't help feeling pleased to be naked in the same room with him, even if he still had his towel on. She fleetingly imagined what he might look like if he took them off.

Was it just her, or was the steam room getting even hotter?

"It's okay," she told him. "I'm not offended. It's *my* fault, after all. *I* took off the towel."

"Are you gonna put it back on now?"

She stared at him, her eyes narrowing slightly. There was something about his question that seemed both teasing and curious. "It's too late. You've already seen all of me."

"Seeing and feeling are two different things," the man told her, angling his head slightly so she could see his smirk. "It's never too late."

Ashley swallowed hard. His words were almost as thick with meaning as his arms were with muscles.

Well, two can play that game, Ashley thought, throwing her hair over her shoulder Putting on her best sultry voice, she said, "It's hot in here. I think I'll stay like this"

He returned his gaze to her, his eyes taking in her entire body at once, rising from her breasts to her face. Those piercing eyes of his finally came to a stop, riveted on her core, and Ashley felt a wetness pool between her legs. Before she knew it, she'd parted them wider.

She'd been expecting the grin on his face, but she wasn't in the least prepared for what came next.

"In that case," the man told her, "I think it's only right that we're…even. You know, just so you don't feel too uncomfortable."

With that, he rose to his feet and tugged on the towel till it came free, pooling around his ankles.

Ashley nearly passed out on the spot. She stared at the towel on the floor for a few seconds, then slowly lifted her gaze. What she saw nearly made her eyes pop out.

He was bigger than she'd imagined, and cleanly shaven. Looking at him, Ashley's jaw nearly hit the floor. His cock was smooth and long and surprisingly thick, the tip of him practically glistening in the light streaming into the steam room. The mere sight of him was enough to make her drool.

Jackpot.

"You can take a picture if you like," he told her, a smirk tugging at his lips. "Then you can stare at it for as long as you like."

"Believe me, I would," she replied, without really thinking. Oh, why hadn't she thought to carry her phone in with her?

"I'm guessing you like what you see." He took a step closer, his eyes fixated on her. "Want to touch me?"

She forced herself to look up at him, swallowing again. She'd never felt this way around Matthew before. Around her husband, she felt pretty normal – bored, even. He simply didn't radiate enough sex appeal. With this stranger…she felt like her insides were going to combust.

Could anyone possibly be a better best friend than Ciara?

Ashley's thoughts flickered to her husband. She really shouldn't be doing this to him. She shouldn't be sitting in here, naked, with a complete stranger. If she knew what was best for her, she'd leave the steam room immediately and never come back.

"Fuck yeah, I want to touch you!"

Without warning, she pulled the man towards her, planting her lips on his before he could react. He didn't stiffen under her touch, but leaned into the kiss, wrapping her legs around his waist so she could feel him pressing against her. His hand reached up and cupped her breast, fondling it, brushing a finger over her distended nipple. Between her thighs, he grew impossibly longer, harder, and Ashley felt herself grow even wetter.

His lips were soft and tasted like salt. He parted her lips with his and slid his tongue into her mouth, circling her tongue with his. Ashley felt his arm wrap around her, pulling her closer to him. When his hand cupped her butt and began to squeeze, she moaned into his mouth, her hands fisting his hair.

It fleetingly occurred to her that someone might walk in and catch them thrashing like wild animals in heat, but Ashley didn't care one bit. She was way too focused on the feel of this man pressing against her to consider what might happen if one of the other people in the gym barged in on them. Besides, Fernandez was cool. He'd let them off the hook, right?

He broke the kiss, gazing into her eyes. "I love your mouth."

"I love that tongue of yours," she replied. She grabbed his head and pulled him back into a kiss. He continued to squeeze her butt, his large hands covering a lot of ground on those rounded cheeks. Ashley briefly wondered what it would feel like to have his fingers inside her, but settled for kissing and holding him. Maybe it was just the intense chemistry between them, but she couldn't help feeling like they had all the time in the world to do whatever they wanted in here.

And Ashley was prepared to experience everything, one after the other.

She felt his teeth scrape across her lower lip, tensing slightly when he nipped at it. In seconds, she relaxed and retuned the kiss with even more fervour. When she laid her hands on his chest and explored, feeling his large pectorals, he let out a soft hiss and the kiss grew hotter. Her fingers slowly traced a path down his chest to his belly, stroking his abs. They really were as hard as they looked, she realised. Like mountainsides sculpted into abs.

Just when she thought she couldn't take any more kisses without practically melting on the spot, the man broke the kiss and put his lips to her neck, nipping slightly at a spot and then sucking hard. Ashley let out a sharp yip and pulled him closer, leaning her head against the wall to give him better access. Tendrils of pleasure pierced through her pores as he began sinking lower, tracing a path of fiery kisses down her neck. Deep down, she felt her pussy hum with anticipation.

"Are you going to eat me out now?" she panted, her eyes fluttering rapidly.

The man stopped kissing her and straightened, smirking down at her. "You'd like that, wouldn't you?"

"You're damn right about that." She spread her legs wider. "Do it before I lose my mind."

His eyes twinkled, but remained where he was, cock stalwart and pointing towards her like a jousting lance. "Beg me."

What? He clearly wanted her just as much as she wanted him. Why was he making this so damn hard for her? If he didn't get those lips and that cock where they were meant to be soon, she was definitely going to lose her goddamn mind.

She bit her lip. If grovelling on the floor was what she had to do to get this man to fuck her, then that was what she was going to do. She pushed her legs even wider. "Pretty please?"

His smirk grew impossibly wider. "Since you said it so nicely…"

He moved towards her, but didn't go down on his knees. Instead, he crashed his lips over her once again. Ashley remained frozen in shock. What the hell was he doing? This wasn't what she'd asked for! Right as she made to protest, she felt his hand slide up her thigh and stroke her swollen clit. Before she could even moan her pleasure, he slipped two fingers inside her.

Fuck. Not even Matthew's fingers had ever been this large. Compared to this guy, Matthew was made out of toothpicks. Clearly, everything about this man was large, Ashley thought, her eyes widening as his fingers pushed in and out of her. She let out a sigh that quickly metamorphosed into an even louder moan, holding on to him as though she might turn into mush if he didn't. Those fingers were doing things to her that no other man's *cock* had ever done. Ashley could feel the pleasure mounting inside her as his fingers picked up the pace. If he kept this up…

She felt a cry building up in her throat as she neared orgasm. In seconds, she was gasping for breath, rocking against the thumb on her clit. The next thing she knew, she'd thrown her head back and was yelling to the tiled ceiling as she came, digging her nails into his shoulders. He kept his fingers inside her and continued to stroke her, even as she covered his fingers with her juices. Finally, he withdrew them and brought them to his mouth, licking his fingertips. A gleam appeared in his gorgeous eyes.

"You're not here for the exercise, are you?" he asked her, amused.

Ashley could be bothered that her cover was blown, that someone already knew the real reason she was here. She could be bothered that things might go wrong and Matthew would find out. Not that Matthew could do much, but she was just really keen on keeping this from him. There was a lot she could be bothered about right now.

But she replied, grinning, "What do you think?"

"I think you taste awesome. What's your name?"

It suddenly occurred to her that they hadn't even introduced themselves, what with the insane heat they'd been creating in the room. "I'm Ashley. And you are…"

"The man who's about to rock your world." He gave her crack a little rub, causing her to gasp. "I think it's time we took this to…the next level. You ready?"

Ashley was nothing if not willing.

3

"Did You Cum?"

Sex with her husband had been a chore, to say the very least. It had been more because *he* wanted it, not because she was any bit interested in having him huff and puff on top of her like a big bad wolf with breathing issues. Ashley needed only to remember the nights she'd spent lying underneath Matthew and wishing he would just be done with it already.

It didn't help that her wishes always came to pass. Matthew never lasted long when they were together in bed. Within minutes, he'd start panting and thrusting erratically, his eyes rolling up into his head like he was about to pass out from the immense strain of fucking for a measly couple of minutes, and then collapse on top of her.

When he asked Ashley if she came, it took all of her willpower not to scream and slap him in the face. *Cum?* It wasn't like he'd even bothered to please her before slipping his dick inside her. Matthew never did foreplay; for some reason, he didn't particularly like it. But that wasn't a good enough reason not to please his wife to orgasm, was it? Ashley understood that he sucked at pleasing her with his dick. Still…she had nothing against being eaten out. But Matthew never considered what she wanted in bed, did he?

She remembered the day she'd decided to put her foot down and make some changes in the bedroom. Matthew had just begun thrusting into her when she placed her hands on his chest to stop him. He'd given her a surprised, somewhat confused look.

"Something wrong?" he'd asked.

Something? Ashley had almost burst into laughter. No, *something* wasn't wrong. *Everything*, every damn thing about sex with him was wrong. But she wasn't going to tell him that just yet. As much as he sucked in bed, he was still a great husband. It wouldn't do to hurt his feelings with the plain truth.

She sucked in a breath. "Will you eat me out?"

Matthew's eyebrows furrowed in a frown. He pushed his brown hair out of his face. "Huh?"

"You know, make me cum with your tongue," she explained, stroking his chest. "I've been hoping to try that out lately."

From the look he gave her, she might as well have asked him to let her give him a chocolate enema. "Why would you want that? Isn't this good enough for you?"

As he spoke, he gave a sudden thrust of his hips, Ashley let out a moan, hoping he wouldn't realise how unusually high-pitched it was.

She grinned at him, sliding her hands lower. "You're right. How about I ride you instead?"

But he wasn't even listening anymore. He'd continued thrusting, moaning into her ear. Ashley sighed into his neck and lay there until he came, two minutes later, groaning her name into her ear. He braced both hands on the bed on both sides of her and planted a kiss on her lips, then raised his head, grinning down at her.

"Did you cum?"

With the steam room stranger, it was a whole different experience entirely. Literally everything about him was enough to make her drip like a leaky tap, from his smile to the way his eyes crinkled, to the size of his cock. When he knelt between her thighs, she thought she just might combust.

"You ready for this, baby?"

His calmness was uncanny. Ashley's chest rose and fell irregularly, her breathing harsh as she replied. "You bet I am."

Oh, what she wouldn't give to have that hot mouth of his on her!

Her breath hitched in her throat when he touched her thighs with his lips, kissing his way up to her drenched pussy. It took all of her willpower to keep from grabbing his head and putting it *there*, right where it belonged. She could only watch him slowly make his way up. He stuck out his tongue, making a trail on each thigh. When he got to the part of her that throbbed the most, he paused, then blew softly on it, causing a shiver to race through Ashley's entire body.

And then he stuck out his tongue…and licked it.

That was more than she could take. Immediately, Ashley let out a sharp cry, and her juices came spurting out of her onto his face. In response, he covered her slit with his tongue, ignoring her cries as he flicked it against her engorged clit. She grabbed his head with both hands and fisted his hair, half trying to push him away, half trying to make sure his head remained where it was. Her orgasm continued to roll out of her, but he continued to please her as if nothing like that was happening.

"Fuck!" she gasped, throwing her head back. This man's tongue was doing things to her that she'd never imagined possible. Not even the many, many vibrators she occasionally used had made her feel this way before. If he kept this up, she might go into shock or something.

Definitely a god.

She began gyrating her hips, her cries growing as the pleasure intensified. The man gave a deep hum, sending vibrations through her, and her eyes rolled up into her head.

"Don't stop," she told him. "Don't you ever fucking stop, you hear me?"

He stopped and rose to his feet.

Ashley stared at him in shock, nearly too weak to move. Her pussy gave a final squirt, the spasms finally dying down inside her.

"What the hell was that for?" she shrieked at him.

In reply, his hand went to his erect cock. "Your turn, baby."

She wanted to get mad at him – but how could she when he'd just given her the best orgasm of her life? Glaring at him, she slid off the bench and dropped to her knees before him, staring up at his face, his cock hovering just inches away from her lips. He wasn't grinning now. The look on his face was serious, yet sexy as hell. When he spoke, he sounded serious, domineering.

"Do it," he commanded.

As if under some kind of spell, she reached up and wrapped her hands around his cock, gasping as she felt just how hot and hard he felt against her palms. And so damn huge! Ashley had never taken a cock this big in her mouth before, but she was willing to try. Anything for this big, gorgeous stranger. Without another moment's hesitation, she licked him at the base of his shaft, running her tongue all the way up to his pulsing head. Then she covered his cock with her mouth and went down on him, taking him in all at once. When his throbbing head hit the back of her throat, she felt tears spring up in her eyes, but she wasn't going to let that stop her. She began bobbing her head up and down his shaft, sucking hard and flicking her tongue around his head every few seconds or so.

"Oh, fuck, Ashley," he grunted, raking his fingers through her hair. She looked up at him and was pleased to see the look of pleasure on his face. His eyes were flickering open and shut at a speed to match lightning, and his mouth hung open in a strangled gasp. Ashley briefly wondered if she'd looked like that while he was eating her out.

Not that it even mattered now, though, she thought as she began jerking him off with her hand, focusing her lips and tongue on his head. Within seconds, he was gasping and moaning, gripping her hair in his fist. She sucked harder and jerked him off faster, then reached for his balls and cupped them, fondling them in her hands. It seemed to turn him on even more, because his grip on her tightened and his cock grew even harder.

"Make me cum, baby," she heard him moan.

Just like that, she released her hold on him and climbed to her feet, enjoying the look of disbelief on his face.

"Two can play at that game," she told him with a wink.

An expression she couldn't quite place flickered across his face, and an unearthly growl erupted from his throat. Before Ashley could react, he grabbed her around the hips and lifted her, wrapping her legs around him. She had only enough time to look at the wild gleam in his eyes before he positioned himself at her entrance and impaled her on his cock.

The feeling was even more intense than she'd imagined. Ashley let out a scream and threw her arms around his neck, bracing herself as he began slamming into her. God, he was so huge inside her. His cock was touching her in places even her largest dildos had never touched, stroking her G-spot like it was nothing. With each pump, she could feel herself drawing closer to an orgasm that would shatter her sanity.

"Oh, my…shit!" she cried as she pounded into her, his hands cupping her buttocks and kneading them. She could feel her breasts jiggling, slapping his chest, tingles racing through them every time her nipples grazed him. "Don't stop fucking me!"

He didn't stop, which she was more than grateful for. The feel of him filling her up with each thrust had her hooked. If he stopped before she could cum…well, a lot of people did crazy things just to satisfy their addictions, right?

Ashley had never had sex this wonderful before. Not even with any of the men she'd been with before she met Matthew. This was something else. She figured it had to do with the heat in the steam room. And then there was the fact that the man fucking her without a care in the world was no novice.

To her surprise, the man slowed down, but before she could protest, he began gyrating his hips in a steady rhythm, grinding his crotch against her so that she felt him brush against her clit. He covered her mouth in a kiss and she moaned into his mouth, feeling her orgasm draw nearer and nearer.

Finally, the insane sensations hit her with the force of a battering ram and she broke the kiss, screaming as she came, her entire body jerking spasmodically as her orgasm shot out of her. The man continued to thrust into her, though slowly now, holding her tight in his arms until her screams died down. Ashley let out a soft moan and placed her hands on his shoulders, leaning in for a kiss.

All of a sudden, he pulled her off him and flipped her around, bending her over on the bench and positioning his cock at her entrance once again. Ashley's eyes widened.

"What are you –?"

"Did you think I was done with you?"

She swallowed. Was she ready to do this one more time? He'd make her cum twice already. One more time and she just might collapse.

He didn't wait for her to respond, but slammed into her again, wrenching a cry from her lips. She gripped the edge of the bench as he pounded into her, his grip tight on her hips. She could hear the grunts coming from him. Somehow, even that managed to turn her on even more and she began shifting her hips to meet his powerful thrusts. The moans in the steam room grew louder and the room grew even warmer. Time itself seemed to slow down.

Then she was coming again, screaming so loudly she was pretty sure pedestrians could hear her all the way from downtown. Her pussy clenched around his cock as her juices rolled onto his cock and out of her, and she felt his strokes become erratic.

Within seconds, he, too, came, yelling her name as he released his seed inside her.

She heard a wet *plop* as he pulled out of her. When she turned and sat on the bench, her chest heaving, she could see him reaching for his towel.

"That…was…marvellous," Ashley panted, feeling her consciousness begin to wane.

Was it just her or was the room growing darker all of a sudden? She could still see the man, though. She saw him turn around and grin, make his way towards her and plant a kiss on her lips. She saw him when he turned back to wrap the towel around him.

His sexy butt was the last thing she saw.

4

"When Next Are You Guys Gonna Fuck?"

How long she'd sat passed out on the bench, Ashley couldn't be sure, but when she came to, she'd found her towel wrapped around her like nothing had happened. For a moment, she wondered if the whole incident with the stranger had been a dream. Then she felt a faint throbbing in the apex of her thighs. It had all been real.

The guy was nowhere to be found, she'd discovered after a quick sweep of the place. He'd had the good sense to put her towel back on her while she was unconscious. And from the look of things, she decided, feeling her cunt, he'd somehow cleaned her up. Wild as he was, he wasn't a complete animal. The thought had brought a smile to her lips.

There was still the other problem, though: she still didn't know what the guy's name was. And she hadn't gotten his phone number. Not that she could have done that while she was passed out or anything, but at least some information about him would've been good. Why hadn't he just left her a note, or written his number on her forearm while she was out, or something? Who did he think he was, fucking her brains out and not even having the decency to drop a phone number for customer feedback?

Still…the sex had been *amazing*. Never before had she passed out from sex. Well, she'd nodded off during one of Matthew's attempts at "making her cum", but that didn't count. This was different. She'd lost consciousness from an orgasm that nearly rid her of her sanity.

Whoever that stranger was, she needed to meet him again – and *soon*.

It was Wednesday evening, and Ashley and Ciara were at the movies, gazing at the big screen from the top row. There were a couple other things Ashley could be doing at the moment – namely, *work* – but she'd decided to take the rest of the day off and hang out with her best friend.

Not that she was having much fun. They were watching a romantic movie Ciara had been dying to see, and every time a passionate scene came on, Ashley couldn't help having flashbacks of what had happened on Saturday in the steam room.

Flash. A man with no name kissing her like she was the last person in the world, her enjoying it more than anything.

Flash. The same man kneeling between her thighs and eating her out, making her explode with pleasure.

Flash. The man shoving his massive cock into her pussy and making her cum again and again.

Blackout.

"Earth to Ashley?"

Ashley blinked and turned to look at her friend, who was gazing at her with a look of confusion and concern on her face.

"Yeah?" she asked as casually as she could manage.

Ciara tossed her brown curls out of her face. "Girl, what are you thinking about? I've been trying to get your attention for the past five minutes now, and you've just been sitting there staring like some genie's showing your future. What's up with you? You've been acting strange since we got here."

Oh, it's nothing too serious, Ashley wanted to say. *Just sex flashbacks from when I fucked some guy in the room you told me to stay away from.*

Ciara still had no idea what had happened on Saturday. She hadn't even asked, which was good because Ashley didn't think she'd have the heart to lie to her best friend. As much as she wanted to tell

Ciara about her sex experience, she wasn't sure what her friend might think.

"I'm fine," she told her, hoping she sounded convincing enough. "Don't you worry about me."

Ciara shot her a look of suspicion for a couple of seconds, then shrugged and faced the screen, jamming a handful of popcorn into her mouth. "If you say so."

The movie went on. It was quite dull, Ashley decided, reaching for the popcorn. A cliché love story: guy falls in love with girl, girl feels the same way and pretends otherwise, dropping little hints every now and then. But the acting was intense. The sex scenes seemed so real, so vivid, Ashley found herself thinking about how real it had felt with the stranger in the steam room…

Wait a minute. What was that pooling between her legs? Was that…?

"Oh, crap," she moaned. This wasn't the time or place to get horny!

Ciara set down the popcorn and turned to face her friend. "Okay, you're gonna have to tell me what's going on with you."

Ashley bit her lip, feeling a look of guilt creep onto her face as she gazed at her fiend. There was no point trying to hide it anymore.

"I can't stop thinking about Saturday," she blurted.

"What happened on Saturday? Ciara's eyebrows rose slowly, realisation on her face. "Oh. What happened? Did you finally get laid?"

The guy seated in front of her turned around and glared at the duo. "Shh, I paid for this movie."

Ciara gave a roll of her eyes and grabbed her friend's arm. "C'mon, let's blow this pop stand."

Once they were outside, she turned to face Ashley, an eager expression on her face. "Tell. Me. Everything. Now."

Ashley heaved a sigh, then proceeded to narrate what had happened at *Dez* on Saturday, leaving out the unnecessary details. Ciara's eyes grew wider and wider until she thought they might just roll out of their sockets. By the time she was done, her mouth was hanging open.

"I don't believe this," Ciara said, practically bouncing the spot with excitement. "You actually did it!"

She turned serious rather quickly. "Tell me about him. What's his name? Where's he from? When next are you guys gonna fuck?"

This wasn't the reaction she'd been expecting, but Ashley was more than fine with it. She bit her lower lip. "*Well*, I never actually got his name or phone number. He left before I could get either."

Ciara looked at her friend like she was the dumbest being in the entire universe. "I don't believe this. You had sex with a hunk and never bothered to get his details?"

"In my defence, getting a phone number isn't exactly what one thinks about while being pummelled by a human drill."

Her friend shook her head and groaned. "Girl, you have got to get your butt back to thc gym and look for him. Make sure you get his phone number this time."

"I'll make sure to do that, ma'am."

Ashley gave a mock salute, causing Ciara to toll her eyes again. They made for the exit, Ashley's mind locking on the mystery man. So she was going to see him again. The thought sent a shiver racing through her. She could only imagine what might go down between them again. Ashley's bones nearly turned to mush at the memory of the man slamming into her from behind, gripping her waist like he was trying not to let her go. What other styles would they try out this time? Reverse cowgirl? The lotus position?

As long as she got his digits beforehand, she was okay with whatever happened in that steam room.

"How's it going with Matthias?" Ciara asked as they headed out of the mall, snapping Ashley out of her thoughts.

"*Matthew*," she corrected. "He's as good as can be. None the wiser. We're meeting with the lawyer next week. I just hope he doesn't find out what I did before it's all over between us."

"It was over between you two from the start," her best friend told her, making a face. "You don't need to worry about him. Just do you – no, do that guy from Saturday."

Both women laughed at her joke. Ashley's thoughts quickly strayed to Matthew. She couldn't help feeling a twinge of guilt at the thought of cheating on him. It was wrong.

Or was it?

***

The Escalade pulled up in front of *Dez*.

"Thank you, Eddie," Ashley breathed, practically flying out of the car. "Remember what I told you last week?"

"You're hanging out with your best friend, in case the boss asks," Edward replied drily.

Ashley could tell he already suspected what was going on, but at the moment, she didn't really care. She slammed the door shut and headed into the building before the driver could pull the car out of sight.

The gym was just as she'd remembered it, only with a couple more women and hairy dudes. Ashley didn't waste her time looking around. Immediately, she made in the direction of the steam room, but she'd just taken three steps when a man stepped into her path.

It was Fernandez, and he was grinning as usual. "Hey, pretty!" he said. "How's it going?"

As much as she'd have been cool with staying and chatting, she couldn't afford to waste time with the manager today. Not when there was a steaming pile of hunk waiting for her in the steam room. She flashed him her best apologetic smile.

"I'm so sorry, Fernandez," she said. "But I need to, uh, go check something out."

With that, she left his presence, leaving a bewildered Fernandez standing in her wake.

She undressed and stashed her belongings, then headed for the steam room, pausing just outside.

Took in a deep breath. Exhaled. Was she really ready for this? What was she even expecting to happen in there? How was it going to pan out?

Tentatively, she pushed the door open and was instantly blasted in the face by a gust of steam. She blinked, trying to clear her vision.

The men in the room blinked, too.

There were about ten of them, all hairy and not at all sexy. They sat on the benches with less room between them than Ashley would have liked. For a couple of seconds, they all just stared. Then one of them cleared his throat.

"You're welcome to join us if you want," one of them said. "We don't bite."

Ashley felt her cheeks burn. "No, thank you."

She shut the door and backtracked, slipping into her clothes at the speed of light, then marched out.

Where the hell was this guy? She looked around the gym. None of the men working out looked like him, not even remotely. Could he have come and gone already? Maybe she'd arrived at the gym too late. With her luck, she'd walked in just minutes after he stepped out.

Ugh. She should have known that this wouldn't work out. Ashley shouldered her bag and was heading out of the gym when Fernandez appeared in front of her, stopping her in her tracks.

"Hey, you're back!" he exclaimed.

"Yeah, and I'm leaving," Ashley replied, miffed.

A look she couldn't place flashed in his eyes. "You can't leave yet! Um, I've got something for you."

She stared at him with narrowed eyes. What exactly was this man going on about? She watched him fish into his pockets and rummage a little, his eyebrows drawing closer and closer in a frown. He must have found whatever he was looking for, because he suddenly broke into a smile. He withdrew a crumpled piece of paper and handed it to her.

"What's this?" Ashley asked, regarding the piece with disgust. It looked just like it smelled: sweaty.

"No idea," Fernandez said honestly. "Some guy asked me to give it to you this morning. Said you'd come here looking for him or something.

The mystery man! With trembling fingers, she peeled open the piece of paper and stared at it.

Written in faint ink, in surprisingly neat handwriting, was a phone number. Right below it was a home address.

5

"WHY DON'T WE DO IT IN YOUR BATHROOM?"

I can do this.

Could she, really? Ashley couldn't seem to stop the jittery feeling that came over her as the Escalade drew closer to the building in which her mystery man lived. And for good reason: the street wasn't all that, to begin with. Not compared to the relatively safe neighbourhoods Ashley was used to. There were people of all ages practically everywhere, walking about, cruising through the streets or just standing or sitting around, smoking cigarettes. A couple of men were laughing loudly at something Ashley couldn't hear. As the car drew nearer, they stopped and turned their heads in her direction, all at once. Suddenly, the atmosphere seemed chillier than usual.

"Right there, please," she told Eddie, hoping he was prepared to zoom out of the street in case things got ugly. She pointed at an apartment building two houses away, where the laughing men sat on the steps, staring at the Escalade.

The driver nodded and pulled up in front of the building, staring at her through the rear-view mirror. He looked more wary than usual. Ashley ignored him. She had other things on her mind. Like what might happen when she saw her mystery man. She had so many questions for him.

She climbed out of the car, doing her best to avoid making eye contact with the men on the steps, and shuffled over to Edward's side. She was still in her workout clothes, and from her last visit to the gym, she could tell just how appealing she must look in them.

"Drive around the block a couple of times if you have to," she told him. With that, she turned and made for the steps leading up into the building.

She'd been expecting the men to block her path, maybe do some wolf-whistling and catcalling, but to her surprise they shifted to let her pass and resumed their discussion. Ashley stepped into the building and immediately made for the elevator, and was dismayed to find that it was out of order. With a huff, she headed for the stairs. She came to a stop on the third floor and waited there, panting heavily. Then she headed over to the first door on her right, marked 303. Had to be him. With trembling hands, she fished out the note and checked to make sure she had the right address. Then she knocked on the door.

Almost immediately, it swung open, revealing her mystery man's gorgeous face. He was just as she'd remembered, only this time he was fully clothed. He had on a grey t-shirt over navy-blue sweatpants and white socks. When his dark eyes settled on her, they brightened and his lips curved into a smile.

"I was starting to think you'd never show up," he said, opening the door wider and stepping back to let her in. "Come on in."

When she saw the street, she'd figured his apartment wouldn't be any better, but trust this man to make everything about him perfect. The apartment wasn't as large as she was used to, but it wasn't too small, either. It was cosy, with neatly arranged furniture and yellow walls. From where she stood, she could see the kitchen and the bedroom, both looking good enough to eat, the bed particularly tantalizing.

"You have a wonderful place," she told him. Wonderful was an understatement.

He shot her a wink. "I'm aware."

Minutes later, they were sitting together on a couch in what she figured was his living room, sipping tea. The couch was comfortable, but Ashley found herself wishing she could sit somewhere else. On him, for example. Weird as it was, she didn't even feel bad for thinking about sex so soon. It wasn't her fault he looked like a sex god.

"So," she said suddenly, turning so she was facing him. "You mind telling me everything now?"

He gave a chuckle. "What?"

"Your name, your age, your occupation – everything. It's not fair to fuck someone and leave her passed out without even bothering to give her your name."

The grin on his face widened. "I'm Jackson. Thirty-two. I'm a software developer working freelance. And I'm single."

"Lucky for me," Ashley said, feeling her nipples poke through her sports bra at the sound of his voice.

Jackson's gaze dropped pointedly, and for a thrilling second, she thought he was staring at her breasts. Then she realised his eyes were locked on her finger. She'd forgotten to take off her wedding ring.

Damn.

"It's not what you think," she spluttered, holding up a hand before he could say a word. "I am married, but I'm getting a divorce already."

Jackson let out a throaty laugh. "I know."

Ashley's eyebrows rose. "You do?"

He nodded. "I could tell last week, in the steam room. You had that look in your eye…like you were looking for something new. I figured your husband was some weak dude who never lasted five seconds in bed."

Oh. That was pretty damn accurate.

"Speaking of which," Jackson went on, "would you like to go for another ride? I'm pretty sure you didn't come here just to talk."

As he spoke, he set down his mug and inched towards her, his lips parted slightly. Ashley never knew when he took her mug from her. Her eyes were on those lips as they drew nearer. Before she could stop herself, she lunged forward and let him cover her mouth with his.

It was just as she'd remembered it, maybe a little more intense. His lips were warm and soft, and she felt herself sighing into the kiss as he set her on her back on the couch. Jackson's powerful arms laid her gently, then his hands began exploring her body from her face to her chest, fondling her breasts through her sports bra. His fingers gave her nipples a little tweak, and she let out a gasp, her body bowing slightly off the couch.

She could feel him pressing against her, his hard-on right against her crotch, causing her to grow even wetter. When he lifted her sports bra, exposing her breasts to the air, she took it as her cue, and slid her hand down his torso, palming his cock. Jackson moaned into her mouth and deepened the kiss, but Ashley wasn't done just yet. She slipped her hand through the waistband of his pants and curled her fingers around him, stroking him slightly.

That did it. With a growl, Jackson broke the kiss and tugged off her bra, then proceeded to take off the rest of her clothing. In a thrice, his clothes were on the floor next to hers. He sat there, naked, the veins in his cock bulging.

"I'm going to fuck you so hard, Ashley," he said parting her legs and positioning himself at her entrance, "you're going to wish you'd never met me."

Like she could ever wish she'd never met him, Ashley thought, throwing one leg over the backrest to give him better access. Jackson entered her slowly, filling her up, and she let out a moan, feeling the sensations erupt inside her. Her inner walls stretched wider and wider as he pushed into her, stopping only when he was completely inside her. He gave a grunt and began pumping, his balls slapping against her butt.

"Holy fuck," Jackson hissed. "You're so damn tight."

Ashley didn't respond. She was too busy trying not to scream. This position was doing things to her that her body could barely take. She just lay there, a hand clamped over her mouth, her eyes brimming with tears of ecstasy, soft whimpers escaping her lips every couple of seconds. Around them, the temperature in the apartment seemed to rise.

Almost like they were in the steam room.

Suddenly, an idea popped into her mind.

"I have an idea –" she started to say, but just then his strokes quickened. Ashley felt the pleasure build up inside her and explode, and she let out an ear-splitting cry as her orgasm tore out of her. Her body shook for a few seconds as Jackson slowed his strokes. When she was calmer, she sat up, a wet sucking sound filling the room as his cock slid out of her. Jackson started to position himself at her entrance again, but she stopped him before he could slide inside her.

"No, wait," she said. "I've got an idea. Why don't we do it in your bathroom? You know, with hot water so it's just like the steam room."

A thoughtful look appeared in his eyes and she could tell he knew this wasn't nearly as good as the steam room had been. It was amazing, sure, but nothing compared to when they were shrouded in steam and immense heat.

"I don't think there's hot water..." A gleam appeared in his eyes. "But I think I'd like to try bathroom sex."

With that, he wrapped his arms around her and lifted her off the couch, rising to his feet himself, and made his way towards what she figured was the bathroom, holding her in a fireman's carry. He gave her bottom a light slap, causing her to let out a squeal, then set her down in the shower, climbing in after her.

"This is nice," she said, as he turned on the water. Immediately, a jet of hot water sprayed her face; she squealed and bent over, and it hit the curve of her back. Before she could straighten, she felt Jackson's hands on her waist. The next thing she knew, he'd slid into her and was pounding like there was no tomorrow.

"Oh!" Ashley cried, grabbing the nearest handhold she could reach to steady herself. Jackson didn't once slow down; he kept slamming into her like a battering ram trying to bring down the Great Wall of China.

It certainly wasn't as mind-blowing as the steam room, but this was awesome, Ashley thought, revelling in the way Jackson filled her, the way the water sprayed onto her back and trickled down her crack and between her legs.

This was what she'd signed up for. This was what she'd been waiting for all these years. Jackson was everything she'd ever needed. It didn't matter that he wasn't very rich; she was rich enough for both of them. He was hot and somehow knew exactly how to make her hot and wet without even really trying. And if she counted the way she'd woken up in the steam room, he was also pretty considerate.

Jackson was, to put it simply, perfect.

"Cum for me, baby," he urged her, reaching up to squeeze her breast. "Cum for Jackson."

His words were her undoing. With a cry that nearly shattered her eardrums, Ashley erupted, spraying him with her juices. Her pussy contracted around his cock, and she heard him give a growl. In seconds, he was slamming into her harder than ever, a deep grunt parting his lips as he spilled his semen inside her.

Jackson gave a couple more half-hearted pumps and eased himself out of her, pulling her into a straightened position and turning her around to face him.

"This is crazy," he said, and he kissed her.

Crazy was just about right. But she'd be damned if she didn't love every bit of it.

6

"I HAD TO TELL HIM."

She and Matthew sat in silence and waited for the lawyer to show up so they could "talk".

It was Friday. The office was large and pretty much the typical lawyer's office: desk lamps, stacks of files, cabinets, and a heavy Oakwood table. On the walls around them were portraits of their lawyer, a gaunt-faced man with round glasses. Looking at the portraits, Ashley stifled a snort. *This* was the guy who was supposed to handle their marriage? He didn't even look like he'd ever been in a relationship.

She looked over at Matthew and felt a twinge of guilt and pity. He was such a good guy. He tried hard to appear macho and unfeeling, but Ashley knew just how fragile this man was. She remembered the expression he'd gotten on his face when she told him she wanted a divorce. She remembered how broken he'd looked, how confused he'd sounded. She'd been tempted to listen to him, to tell him she wasn't going to divorce him anymore, and she would have done that if her resolve hadn't been so strong.

For the next couple of days, he'd been miserable, phoning her every ten minutes or so to check on her, never once hesitating to ask if she'd changed her mind about wanting a divorce, telling her how much he loved her and was prepared to do whatever it took to get her to stay. And when she returned home from work, he'd prepared dinner. *That* had nearly thrown her off balance.

And then the questions had escalated. Before long, Matthew started wondering if she was seeing someone else. Ashley had been so infuriated when he asked her, she'd slapped him across the face and slept at Ciara's for the next couple of nights. With time, Matthew seemed to accept that there was nothing he could do to stop the divorce from happening, but even then he hadn't stopped being nice to her, letting her use his cars and his personal driver.

That had left her confused. Sometimes she wondered if he only did that to make her feel guilty about wanting to divorce him. Ashley couldn't help feeling like Matthew was going to suddenly stop being the nice guy he was very soon. By now, his patience must be running thing.

Still, it didn't matter how he felt. After all, this wasn't Ashley's fault, was it? If only Matthew wasn't such a terrible lover, none of this would be happening. Gazing at him, Ashley tried to imagine having mind-blowing, orgasmic sex with him, the kind she'd had with Jackson in the steam room. It didn't work. Matthew was just….Matthew. He would never be anyone else, certainly not Jackson.

"Why are you looking at me like that?"

Ashley blinked. Her husband was staring at her with a look of confusion and concern on his face.

"Um, nothing." She felt her cheeks burn. "I was just wondering if you were okay."

"I could ask you the same thing," Matthew told her. "A couple of minutes ago, you looked like you couldn't wait to get this over with. Now it's almost like you're having doubts."

"I'm not having doubts," Ashley snapped. Taking a deep breath, she said, more calmly, "I'm not having doubts, Matthew. My decision is final."

Her husband looked crestfallen, but merely nodded. For the next minute, there was nothing but silence, which she was more than grateful for. She continued to gaze around the room, trying to distract herself from the thoughts that plagued her.

It didn't work. She couldn't think about her husband or even look at him without thinking about what she'd done with Jackson. It was absurd. She knew she wasn't to blame for anything, so why did she feel so guilty? It wasn't like she'd left a perfect husband in a perfect marriage just to go searching for some cock. Her husband wasn't *perfect*.

Stop thinking about this, she told herself. It wouldn't do her any good. She just needed to get all this over with and maybe head over to Jackson's so he could eat her out till she lost consciousness. She'd gone days without seeing that gorgeous face of his and was *starved*. At work, she was distracted half the time, and once she'd shut the doors and windows in her office and touched herself to the thought of him until she climaxed. She'd had to wipe her juices off her desk.

Maybe she and Jackson could do it together sometime, in her office after work hours. She'd have to tell him that when she saw him.

Now, where was that damn lawyer?

"You know, when this marriage is over, you're still welcome to come over to my place whenever you want," Matthew told her, breaking the silence.

Ashley refrained from rolling her eyes, just in time. "Matthew, that's not necessary –"

"Yes, it is," he cut in, turning to face her, his eyes filled with a bit of emotion. He reached towards her and laid an arm on hers. "Just because we're getting a divorce doesn't mean we can't be friends, does it?"

"No, it doesn't," she agreed, slowly tugging his arm off hers, "but I think you and I need some space."

She didn't mean to hurt him. A stab of guilt filled her heart when she saw the pain in his eyes.

"Look, Jackson, I –"

Shit.

There was a very pregnant pause. Then Matthew said, "Jackson?"

Ashley gave herself a mental kick. What the fuck was wrong with her?

"That's his name, isn't it?" her husband went on, his expression hardening. Suddenly, he was looking at her like she'd just rolled in horseshit. "*That's* the guy you've been fucking all this time?"

"What on earth are you talking about, Matthew?" she asked, trying to sound confused.

"Oh, don't play dumb with me, you slut," he spat. "I knew something was going on. I knew you were fucking someone on the side."

Ah, there it was: the side of Matthew she'd been anticipating. It was almost amusing how easily it had reared its ugly head. This was the side of him he'd been hiding all those years, while he played nice.

She doubted this new side of him was any better in the bedroom than before, though. He was the same man with the same dick. Just louder and, frankly, more annoying.

Suddenly, anger boiled inside Ashley. He didn't get to talk to her like that.

"And so bloody what?" she asked him. "It's not my fault you can't please a woman in bed. All that money, and you're still not a real man. Of course I had to find someone who could make me feel good."

There was murder in his eyes. "You bitch –"

Just then, the door swung open and the lawyer stepped into the office, clutching a file. He paused, peering over his glasses at the duo.

"Is something wrong?" he wanted to know. "I heard voices."

Ashley forced a smile. "Oh, of course not. We were just arguing sports."

She could tell from his expression that he didn't believe her one bit, but he didn't push further. He walked over to the desk and took his seat, adjusting his glasses so that they rested on his hook-like nose.

"Now," he said, "shall we?"

***

"I know it was you."

They sat in the car outside *Dez*, gazing at each other through the rear-view mirror. Edward looked somewhat timid and confused, but Ashley knew it was all an act. She continued to glare at him.

"I don't know what you're talking about, ma'am," the driver told her.

She smiled, but it never reached her eyes. "If I recall correctly, I told you to tell my husband, if he asked, that I was out with my best friend. Did I not?"

"You did, ma'am."

"So tell me, Edward," she said, leaning forward in her seat, "why Matthew seemed to know the truth about what I was doing, why he was so quick to conclude yesterday."

The driver was silent for a moment. Then: "I had to tell him. He said he'd fire me if I didn't say the truth."

Ah. So he'd been kissing his boss's ass to save his job. Ashley wondered what Ciara would make of all this. Matthew was never supposed to have found out. Now it didn't matter whether they were still married or not. Things were going to plummet very soon; she could feel it in her bones.

"I see," she told him. "Your services for me are no longer required, Edward. I believe I can drive myself from now on."

The driver opened his mouth in protest, but whatever he was going to say, Ashley never heard it. She climbed out of the car before he could speak and slammed the door shut behind her, marching into the building without once looking back.

***

"I knew you'd come," Jackson said to her, his deep voice reverberating off the walls in the steam room. He traced a path up her torso with his finger, circling her breasts in turn and then focusing on her nipples.

By the time he finally touched her left nipple, she was panting heavily.

"You know what I want you to do," she told him.

He tweaked her nipple, making her gasp. "Do I? You haven't told me anything yet."

Ashley swallowed. "I want you to eat me out, then fuck me like I've been bad. I want your hands on my body. I want you to make me cum."

Jackson's lips curved into a grin she knew all too well. "As you wish, baby."

He sank to his knees before her and parted her legs, touching his tongue to her exposed slit, and she let out a cry. Jackson ran his tongue against her clit, flicking faster and harder, sliding one finger into her pussy to stroke her G-spot. Her eye flickered shut and she threw her head backwards, moaning her pleasure to the ceiling.

"Yes, just like that, baby," she encouraged him, squeezing her own nipples so that her pleasure was intensified. She loved the way his tongue felt on her clit, the way he filled her pussy when he inserted more fingers into her pussy and pumped.

In moments, she'd reached orgasm, her moans rising into a shriek as it shot out of her. Jackson grinned at her, gave her cunt a rub for a couple of seconds as she came, trembling like a vibrator in overdrive, and rose to his feet, his cock hard and ready. Ashley wanted to suck it, but before she could voice out her wish, he nudged her thighs apart with his knees and positioned his cock at her entrance. It was hot and pulsed against her, and soon Jackson began rubbing her clit with it.

Ashley let out a moan and held out a hand to stop him. "Just put it in already, dammit!"

Jackson shot her a smirk. Then he shoved into her, filling her up in an instant. Ashley's eyes widened and she gave a squeal as he began his strokes, shoving in and out of her, pumping like a piston. Tendrils of pleasure snaked their way through her, and she could think of nothing else besides the cock inside her and how it made her feel.

"Oh, Jackson, I love the way you feel inside me," she moaned. "You're so big and hot."

"You like that, yeah?" he replied, quickening his strokes so that her eyes bulged. "I think you like how hot and wet I make you."

Of course she did, she thought, gripping the edge of the bench as he continued to fuck her, the wet slapping sounds filling her ears. She was drawing closer to her orgasm; she could feel it hovering nearer and nearer.

Seconds later, it hit her, slamming into her with full force and shooting out of her, causing her body to tremble as the incredible sensations raced through her. Her juices squirted out of her like a fountain, and she cried out until her throat was nearly hoarse.

It took her a little over a minute to calm down. She continued to spasm for some time before her orgasm came to an end. Panting, exhausted, Ashley opened her eyes and gazed around the steam room, heaving a sigh of disappointment. Jackson was nowhere to be seen. Not even the hairy men from last time were in sight. She was still alone – painfully, disturbingly alone.

She let out a sigh and reached for her towel. Jerking off had been fun, but she needed the real thing. And she was going to get him.

7

"Too Early To Think About Romance?"

When she looked back on it, maybe she shouldn't have told Edward what she had. Driving herself around was no fun. If anything, it was a chore. For one thing, the Escalade was too large for her liking. The car seemed…awkward. And then there was the fact that she got distracted easily while driving. It didn't help that Ciara kept texting her every ten seconds.

For the umpteenth time, Ashley pulled over and picked up her phone, reading the message from her friend:

He did WHAT? Girl, you made the right choice divorcing that asshole of a man. He called you a bitch? For Christ's sake, that's real low.

Just then, another message came in: *Where are you?*

On my way to Jackson's, Ashley replied and set down the phone. She pulled the Escalade back onto the road and continued driving.

It had been five days since the incident in the lawyer's office, yet Ashley had only recently filled her friend in on the details. When she thought about it now, she wished she'd told her much later. She appreciated Ciara's concern, but she didn't like how miffed she sounded. Ashley didn't want to make a big deal out of something so trivial, especially since she and Matthew would be divorced pretty soon.

She glanced into the rear-view mirror and did a double take, her eyes narrowing slightly. There was a black Mercedes following closely behind. She couldn't see whoever it was in the driver seat, but the mere sight of the car made her uneasy. Why did the car look so familiar? And why did it seem like she was being…*followed*?

Ashley pushed the thought out of her mind and continued driving. It was probably nothing. This probably happened a lot when Edward was at the wheel. She was just being paranoid.

The drive to Jackson's took a little over twenty minutes, owing to the fact that she kept stopping to check her phone. Ciara had texted her again, telling her to have fun at Jackson's but be prepared to give her a blow-by-blow of her time with him, telling her to be careful in case Matthew decided to try something stupid to get back at her, telling her to make sure Jackson fucked her till she passed out again and then when she woke up.

She brought the Escalade to a stop outside the apartment building and looked in the rear-view mirror. The Mercedes was nowhere in sight. Heaving a huge sigh of relief, Ashley climbed out of the car and made her way up the front steps into the building, waving in greeting at the men who sat there. She headed for the stairs and half-ran, half-flew up to the third floor, not once stopping until she reached the door to Jackson's apartment.

He pulled the door open right before the third knock and grinned when he saw her.

"Hey, beautiful," he said, and her heart gave a flutter.

"Something needs to be done about that elevator," Ashley told him, panting. "I hate having to climb the stairs."

"You know it's worth it." He pulled her into a kiss before she could say anything else, and she nearly melted in his arms. Jackson whisked her into the apartment and shut the door, breaking the kiss.

"You sure you want to do this now?" he asked her. "We could just talk first if you want."

"I've never been more sure in my life," she replied, angling her head so she could get a kiss from him. "You weren't at the gym on Saturday. I missed you."

Jackson inched his face closer to hers, then withdrew it just before their lips could touch. "Pity. I had a lot of work to do then. I hope you didn't wait too long for me?"

Was he teasing her? At this rate, she just might go insane if she didn't get to kiss those lips of his.

"Actually, I spent the entire hour jerking off to the thought of you."

A look of pure amusement crossed his face. "Oh? Did you cum?"

"Twice," said Ashley, trying to pull his face towards hers. "But it wasn't as amazing as I was hoping it would be. I want the real thing. I want you, dammit!"

With that, she pulled even harder, covering his mouth with hers. This time, he didn't resist, and she felt his tongue part her lips and make its way into her mouth, flattening hers in an instant. His lips caressed hers, sending tingles through her body. His hands cupped her butt and he lifted her off the floor, wrapping her legs around his waist. Ashley felt herself being carried away from the spot.

The next thing she knew, he'd flung her onto the bed. Her eyes flew open just in time to see him take off his t-shirt and pants. He got onto the bed and continued to kiss her, peeling off her clothes in a swift, effortless manner that got Ashley wondering how many other women he must have done this with. The thought lingered in her mind for a moment, and she felt a twinge of jealousy. She shoved the thought out of her mind and let him kiss her.

He tugged off her panties and began rubbing her pussy with his fingers, and she let out a moan, reaching down and stroking his cock, rubbing it against her clit. He broke the kiss and straightened above her, parting her legs with a nudge of his hands. He positioned his cock against her entrance and raised his head to meet her gaze.

"Shall I?"

And Ashley was instantly reminded of why she adored this man so much. It wasn't just because of the amazing sex. He was a wonderful person all around, and although he tossed and turned her about in the bedroom like a rag doll, he respected her. She felt a thrill race through her as she nodded, bracing herself for the incredible sensations that would come as he filled her with himself.

Afterwards, they lay naked in bed in the afterglow of their lovemaking, their arms around each other. The apartment smelled of sweaty sex, but neither was bothered about that. Ashley couldn't think about much besides how good it felt to lie in his embrace.

This was only the third time they'd had sex, yet it felt so natural to be with Jackson like this. Almost like they were made to be together, Ashley thought. She couldn't recall ever feeling this way with anyone else in all her years – not even Matthew, and she'd gotten comfortable around him really quickly. Jackson was something else.

Maybe he was the one she'd been looking for all this while. And not just as a sex partner. He obviously had other qualities she loved. When she thought about it, Jackson would make a really good partner for her. The thought put a smile on Ashley's face.

But she'd barely known him long enough to start thinking about things like this, she told herself, wiping the smile off her face. Sure, it felt like he was the one for her, but shouldn't she at least wait some more time before bringing romance into their relationship? As far as anyone was concerned, they were merely sex partners, nothing more. Not even good friends who went out to the movies or had coffee. That was *Ciara*. Jackson was pretty much a sex toy to her – a very sentient, very sexy sex toy.

Ashley couldn't help feeling like he should be more than that to her. Not that it would make a difference if *he* didn't want that.

She gazed up at him and gave a start. He was grinning at her.

"I'd pay a thousand dollars for your thoughts," he said, reaching up to stroke her hair.

Ashley stared at him for a few second, her mind racing. Would it really be wise to tell him what was on her mind? As much as she would love for him to know how she felt now, she didn't want to risk losing what they already had. Then again, wouldn't be better to take that risk than to live on knowing she could never work up the courage to tell him how she felt?

She sucked in a breath. "So I've been wondering…"

"Mmhmm?" He got a curious expression on his face.

"I've been wondering what exactly the relationship is between us," she told him. "You know, if we're just sex partners or…more."

His eyebrows furrowed. "More…as in romantic partners?"

Why did she feel so jittery all of a sudden? She nodded slowly.

Jackson removed his arms from around her and got to his feet without bothering to cover himself. He walked over to the window and just stood there, gazing out. From where she lay, Ashley could see the silhouette of his penis hanging between his thighs like a still pendulum. For what seemed like minutes, he was completely silent.

"You're married, Ashley," he said finally.

She sat up in bed, pulling the sheets up to her chest. "That doesn't matter. Besides, in a matter of days, I'll be happily divorced."

"Regardless, we've only seen each other two, three times. Don't you think it's a bit too early to think about romance?"

Ashley gave herself a mental slap. She'd just *had* to bring up this topic of all topics. And now, what? He'd rebuffed her advances without a second thought. What the hell had she been thinking? He was right: it was too early to be thinking about things like this. This was a sex relationship, nothing more.

She figured she must've gotten so attached because of her crumbling relationship with Matthew. She *had* loved the guy, before he started revealing his flaws in all their glory. And now here she was, catching feelings for a man who didn't want her the way she thought she wanted him.

Get a hold of yourself, Ashley, she scolded herself.

"Hey, what's that car doing there?" Jackson said suddenly. "I swear it wasn't there when you arrived."

What the hell was he talking about? Ashley climbed out of bed and made for the window, peeking around him to see what he was gazing at. Parked right across the street was a black Mercedes.

"What the…?"

And then it hit her. Suddenly, she realised why she'd recognised the car earlier, when it was tailing her in traffic. That was one of Matthew's cars. And she'd be damned if didn't know who it was watching them from the driver's seat.

"I'm guessing that's your husband," Jackson muttered.

There was something different about his voice. Was that…anger? She never had time to reply, because he suddenly left her side, slipped into his clothes and headed out of the apartment, leaving her frozen in shock by the window. A minute later, she spotted him heading across the street to the car, just as Matthew climbed out. To her relief, Jackson didn't attack, but seemed to be asking her husband something.

Good. As much as she would love to see Matthew get what he deserved, she didn't want anything happening to Jackson. Matthew was rich and powerful. All it would take to get Jackson in serious trouble was a little palm-greasing.

A sudden movement caught her eye. It was Matthew, striking at Jackson. To Ashley's dismay, his fist connected with Jackson's jaw, sending the other man reeling backwards.

"Oh!" she gasped, her hands flying to her mouth.

A couple of men raced towards the duo, but by then Jackson had regained his balance. Matthew tried to sock him again, but this time he was prepared. Jackson ducked and launched a punch at his head, knocking him to the ground in an instant. And then the men were pulling him away.

"You stay the fuck away from here!" he yelled, loud enough for everyone within the vicinity to hear.

To her surprise and utmost disappointment, Matthew was still conscious. Ashley watched as her husband climbed to his feet, clutching his head, and half-hobbled over to the car, wrenching the door open and climbing inside as quickly as he could. In seconds, he was speeding out of the street.

The men holding Jackson let go of him and he made his way back towards the apartment building. He looked up, gazing directly at the window where Ashley was, and she felt a sudden surge of emotion.

Was that…was that pride? Why did she suddenly feel so much more attracted to him?

It didn't matter, because a minute later, he came bursting through the door, slamming it shut behind him. Ashley had only time to blink before he grabbed her and kissed her, long and hard. When he finally broke the kiss, there were a million emotions in his eyes. She looked down and saw a massive tent in his pants.

"Get on the bed," he ordered. "Now."

Anything for him.

8

"WHAT?"

For the fifteenth time that night, Ashley glanced up at the clock and let out a groan of dismay. It was ten minutes to eight, and Jackson still hadn't showed up at her office.

A couple of weeks had gone by since the scuffle between Jackson and her husband, and in that time a whole lot had happened. She and Jackson had been arranging meetings in different locations besides the steam room and his apartment. They'd been fucking like a couple of horny rabbits in bathroom stalls in public places, jerking each other off while they were at the movies, and even made each other cum several times over on the desk at Ashley's workplace. And Ashley did not mind one bit.

She loved how much Jackson had changed since he punched Matthew. He'd seemed even more attracted to her than before, which was just as well, because she felt the same way about him. She could tell it had something to do with what had happened that day. The thing was, while she understood why she felt so much more attracted to him, she couldn't quite figure out why he seemed to feel the same way about her. Something about him was different. He was still a sex god, but now he didn't seem so…*detached.* Ashley could tell from the way he often held her on nights when she slept over at his place, the way he smiled at her when he thought she wasn't looking. If she didn't know better, she would've assumed he was already catching feelings for her. But that wasn't possible, was it?

Matthew had been steamed ever since he got knocked to the ground like a sack of tomatoes. Ashley rarely slept over at his mansion anymore, but when she did, she sensed his fury. As much as she tried to act calm about the whole thing, it scared her. Matthew had already tailed her to Jackson's place and picked a fight with him. There was no telling what else this jealous, deranged man was capable of.

She gave the clock another glance and threw her hands into the air in exasperation. Obviously, Jackson wasn't going to show up tonight. Ashley gave a huff. He could've at least called to tell her he was going to bail on her. She'd spent over an hour waiting for him and she was horny as hell.

"Looks like this is a solo mission tonight," she muttered, placing her feet on the desk so that her legs were parted wide. Without another word, she closed her eyes and slid her hand down towards her clit.

***

Thirty minutes and four orgasms later, Jackson still hadn't phoned her.

Okay, something wasn't quite right.

Ashley pulled her feet off the table and cleaned herself up, then reached for the phone, hoping to see a message from him. There was nothing. Her features contorted into a frown. What in the world was going on? How could he just bail on her without even bothering to give her an explanation?

She wished she could get mad at him for this, as much as she tried to, she couldn't. Jackson wasn't the sort of person Ashley could ever dislike or get mad at. And then there was the fact that she suspected something else was wrong. The only other time Jackson had bailed on her without leaving a message had been the day they met, and even then he'd had the decency to compensate for it by covering her up. This was way too unlike him.

She gave his phone a couple of rings, but there was no answer. *Damn.*

Ashley's mind began racing with thoughts, each one worse than the last. What if something had happened to him? What if he'd gotten robbed on his way here? What if…what if he'd gotten involved in a car crash? And here she was, feeling bad that he hadn't showed up to make her squirt.

No. She pushed the thought out of her mind. It wouldn't do to be negative at a time like this. What she needed to do was calm down.

She dialled Ciara, who picked up on the second ring.

"Hey, girl," her best friend said brightly. "What's up? Wanna go see a movie or something? Because I don't think I –"

"No, it's not that," Ashley told her, her voice laced with panic. "Jackson and I were supposed to, you know, hook up tonight at my office. But he's two hours late and he won't pick up his calls. I'm getting worried."

There was a pause on the other end of the line. Then Ciara said, "I'm pretty sure it's nothing. He probably got stuck in traffic or something."

"For *an hour and a half?*"

She could practically feel her friend shrugging on the other end. "I've sat in traffic for three hours, girl. Ain't nothing strange about that. Look, there's no need to worry about Jackson. I'm sure he's fine. You make it sound he must've gotten attacked. Is there something I should know about?"

Ashley bit her lip. Of course there was. But she hadn't even bothered to give Ciara the gist, not for two weeks. She gave herself a mental slap. What a great best friend she was.

"I don't know," she said with a sigh. "Does the fact that he got into a fight with my husband a couple of weeks ago count?"

"*WHAT?*"

Ciara launched into a string of expletives that could've cost her a tongue in different circumstances. On the other end, Ashley clutched the phone to her ear and tried not to cringe. When her best friend finally calmed down, she explained everything that had happened on that day. By the time she was done, there was complete silence on Ciara's end.

"Hello?" Ashley tried.

"I'm still here," Ciara replied. "This is really bad. It doesn't matter if Matthew deserved it or not. That guy is rich. He could do whatever just to make sure Jackson suffers. Oh, why didn't you tell me about this much sooner?"

Ashley swallowed slightly. "I –"

"Don't worry about that," her friend said, cutting her short. "What you need to do is go home and find out if Matthew has something to do with Jackson ghosting on you. I'll see what I can do from my end. Just try to be careful."

Ashley didn't like the way Ciara had said *ghosting* – as if Jackson was dead or something – but she tried to remain calm. She said goodnight and hung up, staring blankly out her office window into the night.

Something was wrong with Jackson, and she wouldn't put it past Matthew to be involved in it. She hoped her hunch was wrong, then the door would swing open any moment and Jackson would saunter in with that sexy smile on his face, apologising for being so late by taking her on her own desk.

But deep down, she knew just how right she was.

***

When Edward had been her driver, he'd always been respectful of traffic regulations and never drove any faster than he was comfortable with. The trip from the office to Matthew's mansion had always taken fifteen minutes when he drove her.

Ashley got there in five.

She weaved through the streets like a madwoman, honking every ten seconds as she careened in and out of the opposite lane, ignoring the angry yells and the middle fingers the other motorists flashed at her. Once or twice, she nearly crashed headfirst into another speeding vehicle, but somehow she managed to keep from dying. By the time she pulled up in front of the mansion, her heart was pounding against her ribcage, threatening to burst free.

Matthew's Mercedes sat parked ten feet away. That meant he had to be home. *Good* She needed to have a nice little chat with her husband. She climbed out of the Escalade and made her way into the house, her handbag dangling precariously from her clenched fist.

"Matthew?" The waiting room was empty, obviously. He wouldn't sit in there even if he was expecting her, which she doubted he was. Ashley headed into the living room, then the kitchen. Both were also empty. Where the hell was this man? "Matthew?"

There was no reply. Ashley could feel her impatience grow. She needed to find her husband, find out what he'd done to Jackson. She needed answers now!

"Matthew, where the fuck are you?" she yelled, her voice echoing through the house.

Why did it feel so empty?

She decided the bastard must be upstairs in the bedroom. No doubt, he was asleep already. Ashley didn't care. She'd punch him awake if she had to. She made her way upstairs to the bedroom and was shocked to find he wasn't there, either. As far as she knew, he wasn't anywhere in the house.

Okay, what the fuck was going on?

He must have driven one of his other cars, she figured, slapping her forehead. She plunked down onto the bed and sank her head into her palms. Matthew wasn't even home yet. She was going to have to wait.

At what point she fell asleep, Ashley wasn't sure, but when she awoke, her husband was standing over her, a slightly amused look on his face. She glanced around quickly. She was still in his bedroom. It was morning now. She must've slept all night.

"Nice of you to drop in," Matthew said. He was all dressed up, though his suit had a wet stain on the lapel. His hair was tousled and his eyes bloodshot. Ashley figured he'd just returned from wherever he'd been all night.

She rubbed her eyes, trying to get the sleep out of them, and suddenly one thought filled her mind. *Jackson.* Immediately, she was on her feet, the details of last night rushing back to meet her. She fixed her husband with a glare.

"What did you do to Jackson?" she snapped.

The look of amusement on his face grew even more prominent. He gave a shrug. "Nothing he didn't deserve."

She grabbed him by the collar of his shirt, which wasn't easy considering he was taller than she was. "Tell me what you did!"

Matthew gave a sigh. "Fine. I had him arrested and put in a cell."

9

"SHE ISN'T JUST A TOOL FOR MASTURBATION"

Arrested. The word reverberated through Ashley's mind and she let go of his collar. For a few seconds, she just stood staring at her husband in shock. She nearly went weak in the knees as the thoughts consumed her.

He'd had Jackson arrested. But Jackson hadn't done anything wrong. He was not a criminal, as far as he knew. He didn't even seem like the kind of guy who'd want to commit a crime. Jackson was a kind and considerate person, to say the very least. Why on earth would Matthew have him put in jail? And how...?

It hit her with the brute force of a sledgehammer. *Of course.* Suddenly, she remembered the night he and Jackson had had that little brawl. Clearly, the humiliation hadn't left Matthew's mind one bit. Ashley figured he must've bribed a couple of policemen to bring Jackson in for some made-up crime. It didn't help that Jackson was black. Between that and the large amount of money Matthew had to have slipped them, the police must've thrown Jackson into the nearest cell without a second thought.

In that moment, Ashley felt a wave of emotions cascade over her. She felt guilty for having initially treated Jackson's absence like a trivial occurrence, tossing off while he was in a cell. She felt worried at the thought of all the things that could possibly happen to him. Most of all, she felt angry that her husband had gone to this length just to get back at her for cheating on him. As if it wasn't all his fault to begin with.

"You bastard," she seethed. Suddenly, she let out a shriek and shoved him in the chest, sending him stumbling backwards. "You bastard!"

There was a split-second in which pure, unfiltered rage filled Matthew's eyes, but he remained where he stood. "I did what I had to do, Ashley."

"No, you did what you thought would satisfy your bruised ego because you couldn't live with the fact that a better man beat you up." Her breathing was growing harsher by the second. "You did it to get at me!"

Her husband gave a laugh that didn't quite reach his eyes. "You say it like I had no reason to. For fuck's sake, Ashley, you cheated on me with that asshole!"

Asshole? She nearly burst into laughter. That word didn't quite qualify Jackson. There was only one person it fit perfectly, and he was standing right in front of her.

"You know, it's funny how you make all of this sound like it's my fault," she said, her voice low but not at all soft. "Hilarious, even. You continue to say it like I was benefiting anything from this marriage before I started sleeping with Jackson. News flash: I wasn't."

Matthew's jaw clenched. "You were enjoying my money. You were enjoying my love and passion. I always treated you like you were all I had."

This time, she did burst into laughter. Her husband looked at her as though she might be going insane.

"Matthew, I have my own money," she told him. "I'm not worse off without it. What you call love was just a façade – look at you now, acting like a total jerk. And passion? Honey, you were never passionate. Not in the bedroom, that was for sure. And *that's* why I had an affair."

He opened his mouth to speak, but she held up a hand, shutting him up instantly. Ashley thought she heard a sound from somewhere in the house, but she was too riled up to care just yet.

"For years, I endured your poor bedroom skills," she went on. "I wasn't in the least comfortable with the way you fucked. You saw the signs – I was practically holding up a billboard with the words I'M UNCOMFORTABLE written on it – but did you pay attention to them? Did you ever pause to think, 'Maybe my wife is right. Maybe I should listen to her and try to be better in bed, maybe I should actually try to give her what she wants since sex is a *two-way* thing and she isn't just a tool for masturbation, maybe I should actually try lasting twenty measly seconds in bed before coming inside her'?"

"Alright, that's enough," Matthew snapped.

But Ashley was just getting started. She tossed her blonde locks over her shoulder. "You were never a great lover, Matthew. You are nothing but a jerk who claims he's been nothing but awesome to his wife, and in all honesty, no day goes by when I don't regret marrying you in the first place. I'm glad I met Jackson when I did. And I'm more than happy to say that he's more than ten times the man you'll ever be."

Pure rage flashed in Matthew's eyes again. Ashley never saw his hand move, but the next thing she knew, there was a sharp sting as his palm connected with the side of her face and sent her sprawling to the floor. Right before her head hit the tiles, memories flashed through her mind.

She remembered the day he'd promised never to hit her, on their honeymoon. It wouldn't do well for a man to hit a woman, he'd said. Doing so would be an act of cowardice. His words had sent a thrill through Ashley, and her heart had given an extra thump.

"You could always hit me when we're in bed, though," she'd told him with a wink, snuggling closer to him on the king-size bed. "Spank me when I've been a bad girl."

She'd been expecting him to grin and nod in agreement, and was disappointed when his eyes widened in horror.

"No, of course not," he'd told her. "I could never hit you."

This was the same man who'd just struck her like she was nothing. Was there anything consistent about Matthew besides his poor sexual performance?

That was all the time she had to think, though. The next thing she knew, he'd started kicking her, his shoes sending stabs of pain into her thighs. Ashley let out a scream, knowing it was pointless, knowing there was no one who could possibly help her.

Maybe all of this was *her* fault, after all. She'd made a mistake marrying this man.

Just then, a thundering of feet reached her ears. A second later, the bedroom door crashed open and a large figure slammed into Matthew, knocking him to the floor. Before her husband could get back on his feet, the figure was on him, punching him wherever his fists could reach. Now it was Matthew's squeals filling the bedroom. Ashley remained where she was, cowering in terror.

"Don't you *dare* touch her again!" said Matthew's assailant, punching him in the jaw. "You hear me? Don't you ever lay you filthy hands on her!"

Why did that voice sound so familiar?

Suddenly, it hit her. Ashley's eyes widened and she pulled herself into a sitting position.

"Jackson?"

The man froze in mid-punch and glanced over his shoulder at her. Sure enough, it was Jackson, his expression livid as ever, the veins in his neck pulsing like they were about to pop. He panted heavily as he climbed off Matthew, who was now groaning in pain on the floor.

Jackson made his way over to her and helped her to her feet. "You okay?"

"Somebody get me an ambulance," Matthew moaned, clutching his face.

Ashley ignored him. "I'm fine. Thanks for coming to rescue me. Speaking of which, how did you –?"

"Get out of jail?" Jackson managed a small smile. "A woman came to get me out. Somehow, she knew to come looking for me. She may have heavily tipped the policemen, and they dropped the charges against me and let me go. The woman didn't even let me thank her. She just told me I had to get to you immediately, then gave me your home address."

She gave a frown. "But how did she know…?"

Ashley trailed off as realisation slowly dawned on her. "Did this woman by any chance have curly brown hair?"

"Yes." A look of surprise crept onto his face. "How'd you know that?"

"She's my best friend Ciara," she told him, unable to stop the grin that appeared on her face. "I phoned her yesterday when you didn't show up at the office like we'd planned."

She was going to have to specially thank Ciara for her help. That woman had recommended the gym where she met Jackson, and now *this*? If Ashley had her way, Ciara would receive a medal of honour or a key to the city, whichever she could lay her hands on. Damned if that woman wasn't the best of best friends.

Ashley faced Jackson, beaming at him, waves of emotion cascading over her as she gazed into those eyes of his. She felt her heart beat faster as he held her, inching his face closer to hers. Still curled up on the floor, Matthew chose that moment to speak.

"I'm gonna have you both arrested," he groaned. "You and your fucking whore."

Ashley wasn't sure which of them he'd called a whore, but that didn't matter one bit to Jackson. His expression hardened suddenly and, letting go of Ashley, he made his way over to Matthew. Before the other man could utter a word, he'd punched him in the face again. Matthew's eyes rolled up into his head as he lost consciousness.

Jackson walked back to her and held her again, pulling her closer to him. When their lips finally made contact, she felt fireworks exploding in her chest. And of course, there was the inevitable wetness in the apex of her thighs.

She broke the kiss, breathing hard. "I want you to fuck me."

He raised an eyebrow at her. "In here? There's a man passed out at the foot of the bed."

"I know," she told him. "But I'm dying to have you inside me again."

Jackson's lips twitched, then curved into a smile. "Your wish is my command."

With that, he lifted her into his arms and made for the bed, dumping her upon it in a most undignified fashion. Before she could move, he was on her, kissing her like he was under a spell, and she kissed him back, her arousal mounting. Ashley felt his powerful arms encircle her, pressing her body against his. He broke the kiss and began caressing her body with his mouth, kissing her through her clothes. All Ashley had to do was reach down to feel the warm wetness than had already seeped through her panties and soaked her pants.

Before she knew it, he'd taken both their clothes off. How in the world he'd managed to do that without her even really realising it, she didn't know, but she didn't really care, either. Ashley watched as he flung the clothes over his shoulder; she figured they must've landed on Matthew. Jackson hovered above her, gloriously naked and looking good enough to eat. When he started to caress her body with his fingers, all the way down to her dripping crack, she thought she might die with pleasure.

Finally, he positioned his cock at her entrance and pushed slowly into her, filling her up until she moaned her pleasure. Jackson began his strokes, pumping in and out of her, gradually increasing his pace so that her moans rose to cries and then to screams. Once or twice, he leaned down and kissed her, then paid attention to her breasts, suckling on her nipples, and she could feel herself drawing nearer to her release. As she finally tumbled into her third orgasm, a single thought filled her mind:

Jackson was the right man for her.

10

"SHUT THE FUCK UP"

The next few weeks were a near blur to Ashley. It was a miracle she didn't lose her lunch.

The day after the incident with Matthew, she dialled Ciara and asked her friend to meet her for lunch at a nearby café. When the two women met, there was silence for the first ten minutes, and they both just sat and sipped coffee, Ashley poking at her fries with her index finger. Finally, Ashley broke the silence.

"These past few weeks have been pretty weird," she said, staring at her food. In the periphery of her vision, she thought she saw Ciara smile.

"You don't say. Not that I can relate to that much, though. You're the one who went through all that…whatever it was."

Ashley sipped her coffee and set her mug slowly back on the table, her fingers still curled around its handle. "Yeah. To be honest with you, I'm still really shaken."

After their lovemaking the day before, Ashley and Jackson had lain in bed for another hour while Matthew remained unconscious at the foot of the bed, then dressed up and called the police. When she narrated everything that had happened, they'd been surprised and confused. Even more, they were reluctant to arrest Matthew. Ashley wasn't sure whether it was because he was rich and powerful and had begun hurling threats at them the instant he regained consciousness, or whether it was simply because one of the parties in the incident was a black man. Be that as it may, she stood her ground until Matthew was led away in handcuffs and the cops asked the duo to come with them to the station to make a statement.

She couldn't have been happier to know that Matthew was going to jail. After all he'd done, it was just what he deserved. That, and another beating from Jackson, though Ashley didn't think the cops would ever allow that. But Matthew's arrest wasn't enough. They were still married. Luckily, in a week, all of that would be over. No more Matthew breathing down her neck.

But she might not even be alive to enjoy it if it hadn't been for Jackson. If that man had not stepped in when he had, there was no saying what Matthew might've done to her. Beaten her unconscious? Raped her? Drawn a line across her neck with a kitchen knife? One thing was certain to Ashley: she owed him her life. And she owed Ciara for what she'd done to help.

"Sometimes, I wonder where I'd be without you," she told her friend. "You saved my life yesterday, you know that? And you helped bust Jackson out of jail."

Ciara gave a dismissive wave and snagged a fry from Ashley's plate. "Oh, stop being so cheesy."

"But it's true," Ashley said. "You were right about Matthew from the start. Plus, you told me to go to the gym, and that's where I met Jackson."

"To be fair, I didn't know he was going to be there. I never even knew he existed until you told me."

"Yeah, but you led me out of a boring, fruitless marriage and showed me the way to fun."

"That's ridiculous –"

"Would you shut the fuck up for one second and accept the fact that you're an amazing person?" Ashley snapped.

Both women stared at each other for a couple of seconds. Then they burst into laughter.

"I'm so lucky to have you as a friend," Ashley told her, and she meant it with every fibre of her being.

Ciara gave a roll of her eyes, but she was grinning. She raised her coffee mug. "To being the greatest best friends ever."

Ashley raised hers as well. "To being the greatest best friends ever."

They clinked glasses and drank, Ciara spitting the coffee back into the mug almost immediately.

"This tastes like sawdust," she said, making a face, while her friend threw her head back in laughter.

The duo continued chatting for a couple more minutes, then decided to head out and go see a movie. After that, they headed to a bar and had drinks. By the time they headed back to her place that night, both women were nearly completely wasted. Ashley passed out on the couch almost immediately.

As the next few days rolled by, she grew more and more excited, anticipating the day when her marriage to Matthew would be dissolved. And then it was all over, more suddenly than she'd imagined. Ashley couldn't help feeling like a large weight had just been plucked off her chest. Now she was even more free to do whatever she liked, with whoever she wanted.

Not that she would want just *anybody*, though. There was only one man who came to mind whenever she thought of hooking up with someone. And over the next couple of days, she couldn't seem to stop thinking about it.

Ashley couldn't help wondering whether their relationship was purely sexual, whether it had escalated into something much, much more. She remembered what he'd said to her in his apartment, the day he'd first punched Matthew: *Don't you think it's a bit too early to think about romance?* Well, was it still too early? Did it even matter how early it was if they didn't feel it *was* too early?

She'd tried talking to Ciara about it, but for the first time, her friend didn't seem to have an answer. Ciara had been equally confused.

"To be honest, you guys have a weird relationship going on," she'd said. "You're supposedly fucking casually, but then he seems to be more involved in your life than a normal casual sex partner would be, fighting for your sake and all that. I'm sorry, girl, but this is one problem I can't help you with. It's got me stumped as a damn tree."

When she thought about it, though, Ciara had a point. Not about her being unable to help out with Ashley's problem, but about the fact that Jackson seemed unlike the regular casual sex partners. She'd seen the unbridled fury in his eyes when Matthew had hit her. She'd seen how mad he looked when Matthew hit him. Jackson acted like all he wanted from her was sex, but what if there *was* more to it than he claimed? Any moron could see that he cared for her.

Still, it didn't matter, if he wasn't interested in anything beyond a purely sexual relationship. Ashley couldn't force it on him if he didn't want it.

She let out a sigh and walked into the gym.

Naturally, every head within thirty feet of her swivelled in her direction, some lingering on her, but she wasn't in the least fazed. When Fernandez came over to meet her, his grin broad as usual, she smiled back at him.

"Ah, Ashanti," he said. "So nice to see you here again."

"*Ashley,*" she corrected. "Uh, Fernandez? My eyes are up here."

He lifted his gaze off her boobs, his face reddening. "Huh? Oh, yeah. How are you?"

She smirked at him. "To be honest, I'm not sure. Anyway, it was nice to see you again. I'm heading off to the steam room."

"You do that." He nodded in agreement. "It's still empty, though. That guy Jackson? He hasn't showed up yet."

It took a couple of seconds for his words to sink in. Ashley froze, staring at him in shock. He knew!

"Try not to mess up the place," he whispered. "Have a nice afternoon."

With that, he left as though nothing had happened. Ashley stared after him for a moment, then headed for the steam room.

As she undressed and entered the room, wrapping her towel tightly around her, she remembered what Fernandez had said to her, and a smile crossed her face. Did he really think she'd come here to see Jackson? Ashley would've phoned Jackson if she wanted to meet up. She hadn't come here to have sex. She'd come here to think.

She took a seat on a bench in the corner and gazed around the room. This was the first place where she'd met Jackson, the first place they'd had sex. Being in here reminded her of him, of the fun times they'd had. She could still remember the shock and embarrassment she'd felt when she removed her towel only to discover that she wasn't alone in the room. The thought made her grin. She'd been so dumb back then.

But that was the past. It was all gone now. She needed to think about the future now. Did she really have a future with Jackson? Was it just going to be constant sex? As much as she enjoyed that, she couldn't help feeling things could be a lot more than just that. Or maybe things didn't have to continue between herself and Jackson. Maybe she could meet another guy in another steam room. Edward *had* said that there were better gyms in the city. She could always check them out, have sex with whoever she wanted. It wouldn't even have to be anything more.

Another sigh escaped her lips and she leaned back, resting her head on the tiles. Never had she felt so confused and indecisive before.

Don't you think it's a bit too early to think about romance?

Maybe he was right. Maybe it *was* too early.

Just then, the door swung open. She was no longer alone.

Great. Just what she needed.

A silhouette of a woman walked in, a white towel draped around her shoulders and waist. She couldn't see her face clearly through the steam, but she could tell she was curvy. If Ashley hadn't been so deep in thought, she might even have lingered on that. She watched, only half-interested, as the woman took her seat on the bench opposite her.

Her eyes narrowed suddenly. *Wait a minute.* Was she…was she taking off her towel?

She could see the shape of her breast through the steam, and they were perfectly rounded with perked nipples. Nipples hard enough to make her jaw drop. Clearly, the woman had no idea she was here, because she began stroking her breast, moaning softly as she did.

"Oh, Ashley," she moaned. "I want you so bad."

Ashley froze on the spot. She couldn't possibly know she was here. Did that mean she was caressing herself to the thought of her? How did she even know her name?

Suddenly it hit her. Why this woman seemed to know her name. Why she was so sexy. Why she had such beautiful breast. Why her voice sounded so familiar.

"Now, there's something you don't see every day," she said with a smirk.

Ciara leapt to her feet with a yelp of surprise, her towel pooling around her ankles. It took all of Ashley's willpower to keep from bursting into laughter right then and there.

"What's the matter, baby?" she said, still smirking. "Did I interrupt your little session?"

She regained her composure pretty quickly, and broke into a grin. "I should've known you'd be in here. You caught me."

"I did."

She drew closer to her, her breast aiming. "And you heard what I said."

What she'd said?

Suddenly, her words came rushing back to meet her: *Oh Ashley, I want you so bad.* For a couple of seconds, Ashley was struck dumb. She wanted her? She couldn't possibly have faked that if she'd thought she was alone in the room. Did that mean…?

"Yeah, I heard what you said," she told her. "Did you mean it?"

"That's up to you. I think we can discuss that…later. There's plenty of time. For now, though…"

Without warning, Ciara yanked Ashley's towel off, baring her body. Before Ashley could react, Ciara covered her mouth with a kiss, her hands caressing her until she moaned.

Ciara's fingers aimed downward towards Ashley's swollen clit, gently circling her tip.

Ashley's thighs quivered as they slowly parted, Ciara's fingers softly slid inside Ashley's dripping wet pussy. Ashley cried as she moaned Ciara's name "Oh, Ciara, you feels so good inside me". Ciara eased her fingers out of Ashley's wetness and placed them in her mouth as she moaned, "Mmmm your pussy's so sweet". Ciara sat on the bench with her hot pussy in Ashley's face. Ashley leaned in to Ciara's open thighs, eyes closed with her tongue leading the way. A gentle kiss, then a lick, Ashley begins French kissing Ciara's pussy. Ciara pulls Ashley's head into her as her best friends tongue goes deep inside. "I wanna cum, Don't stop Ashley". Ashley moans with her tongue still inside sending Ciara in to uncontrollable spasms. Ashley aggressively continues tongue fucking her. "harder, Spank my ass and pull my nipples", Ashley shouts!

Jackson was two seconds from opening the steam room door but waited while listening to Ashley's voice panting and saying "harder, harder, spank my ass". Jackson slowly pulled the door open, crept in silently while removing his towel. He could barely see through the steam a silhouette of a woman on her knees facing another woman sitting on the bench. Ciara could see Jackson approaching Ashley from behind. "you want me to spank you harder huh?" Ciara suggested. Ashley replied *"yes, harder baby, harder"!* Just then Jackson kneeled behind Ashley giving her firm ass slaps. Ashley pulls her own nipples harder and harder thinking of how Jackson had done it. "I wish Jackson was here with us", Ashley moaned. Just then Jackson leans towards Ashley's ear and whispers, "I'm right here baby". A stunned and shocked Ashley gives a quick look over her shoulder and see's her dream, Jackson. He firmly grabs his thick black shaft and slides it inside Ashley's oozing hot spot. "Oh, Jackson, Oh baby, fuck me," Jackson began thrusting into Ashley while leaning forward towards Ciara's lips. Ciara lifted her arms, pulling Jackson closer and began kissing him while he was penetrating Ashley. With her tongue in his mouth, Ciara say's "fuck her pussy good, Mmmm, fuck her Jackson". Ashley's pussy juices are squirting out of her like a fountain. " I gotta have some now!" Ciara says, while dropping to her knees and laying under Ashley's pussy. Ciara opens her mouth as Ashley's cum squirts inside. She licks Ashley's clit as Jackson's shaft slides in and out. "Suck my balls baby," Jackson groans. Both woman rise and turn to Jackson's cock, Ciara strokes his dick while holding the back of Ashley's head, feeding her his rod. Ashley sucks it faster and faster while Ciara goes back and forth between licking his balls and sucking Ashley's nipples. Ciara and Ashley's fingers are inside each other's wet pussy while Jackson's hands are massaging their breast. In one swoop, Jackson lies on the bench directing Ciara to sit on his cock and Ashley to straddle his face. Ciara hovers above Jackson's rock hard shaft as Ashley sits on his stomach with her hands guiding his cock into Ciara's throbbing pussy. Ciara turns a slow grind into a full ride em cowgirl. The two women lock lips tongue kissing and fondling each other's breast. Jackson pulls Ashley's waist towards his face with his tongue longing to taste her. Ashley gently rests on his face as his tongue enters her pussy. With Ciara riding his cock Jackson buries his face inside Ashley vibrating his lips on her clit. "I'm cumming" moans Ciara, as her silky white cream rolls down his shaft. Jackson

Licks Ashley faster and faster, "I'm gonna cum right now Jackson, don't stop baby, don't stop". Ashley gyrates her hips as her thighs quiver. "Oh Jackson, baby *"I'm cumming, I'm cumming on your face"!* Ashley's pussy explodes with warm cream filling Jackson's mouth dripping down his face. Ciara and Ashley quickly stand Jackson, kneeling at his feet, they jerk and suck his thick cock until he's almost unconscious. *"Oh, Oh shit, I'm gonna cum"!* Just then Jackson's steel volcano erupted, showering his two beauties with his pearl white rain.

www.ingramcontent.com/pod-product-compliance
Lightning Source LLC
Chambersburg PA
CBHW061745050726
47598CB00002B/591